3/05

Tomie dePaola

Mice Squeak, We Speak

A Poem by Arnold L.Shapiro

PUFFIN BOOKS

Cats purr.

roar·roar·roar·

Lions roar.

Owls hoot.

Bears snore.

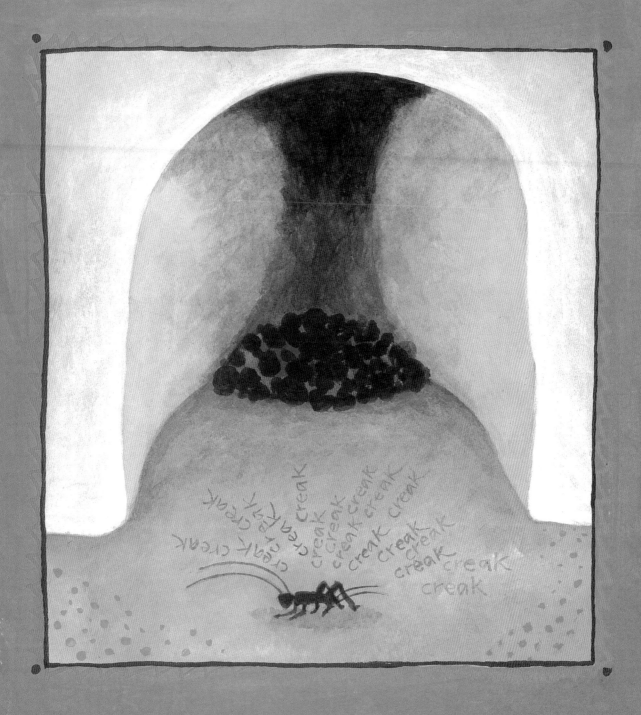

Crickets creak.

Mice squeak.

Sheep baa.

Monkeys chatter.

Cows moo.

Ducks quack.

Doves coo.

Pigs squeal.

Horses neigh.

Chickens cluck.

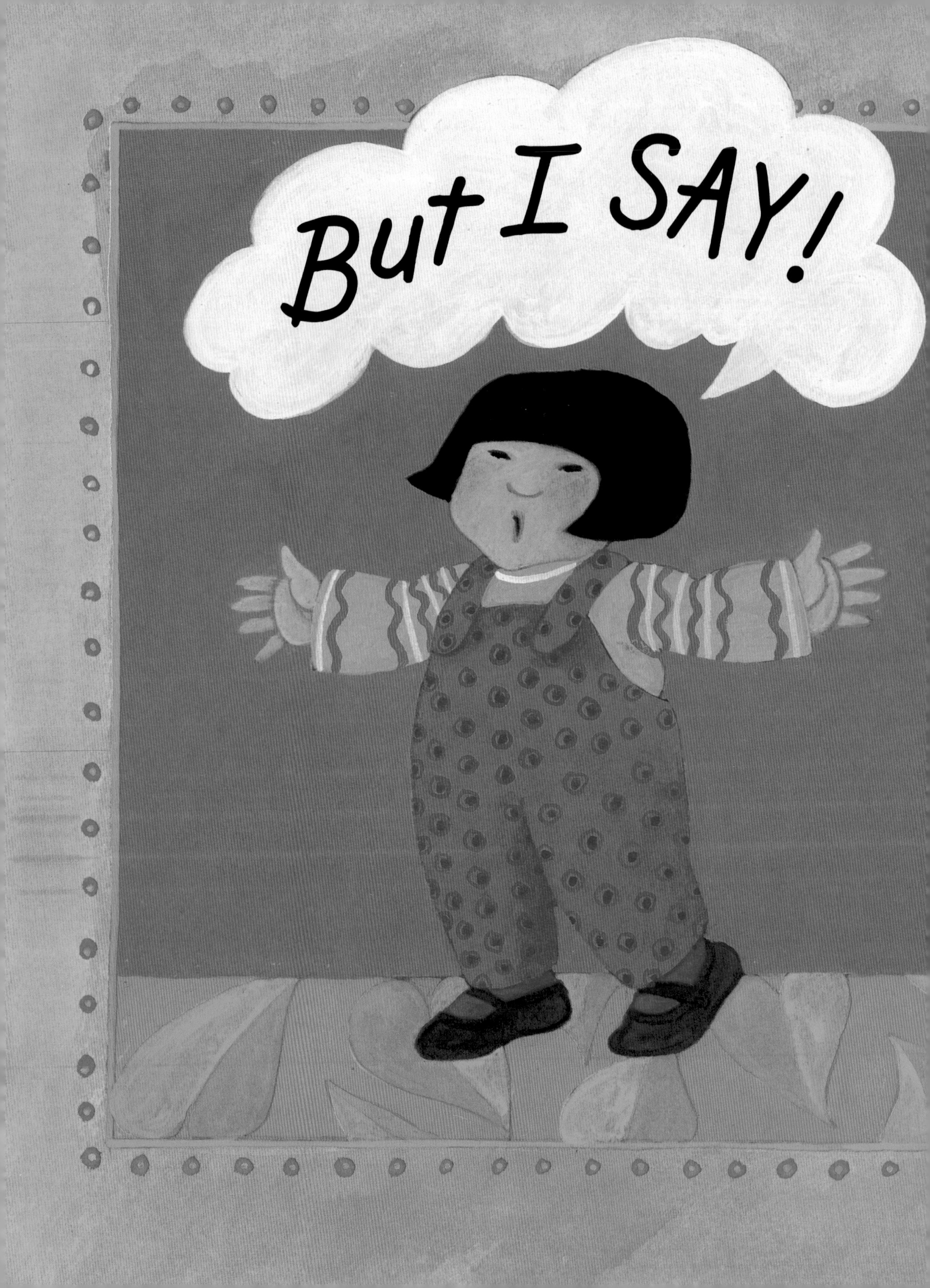
But I SAY!

Flies hum.

Dogs growl.

Bats screech.

Coyotes howl.

Frogs croak.

Parrots squawk.

buzz· buzz· buzz· buzz·

Bees buzz.

For Fraser Anthony

my Aussie godson

and his Mama and Papa, Jenny and Tony

PUFFIN BOOKS
Published by the Penguin Group
Penguin Putnam Books for Young Readers, 345 Hudson Street, New York, New York 10014, U.S.A.
Penguin Books Ltd, 27 Wrights Lane, London W8 5TZ, England
Penguin Books Australia Ltd, Ringwood, Victoria, Australia
Penguin Books Canada Ltd, 10 Alcorn Avenue, Toronto, Ontario, Canada M4V 3B2
Penguin Books (N.Z.) Ltd, 182-190 Wairau Road, Auckland 10, New Zealand

Penguin Books Ltd, Registered Offices: Harmondsworth, Middlesex, England

First published in the United States of America by G. P. Putnam's Sons, a division of The Putnam & Grosset Group, 1997
Published by Puffin Books, a division of Penguin Putnam Books for Young Readers, 2000

5 7 9 10 8 6 4

Illustrations copyright © Tomie dePaola, 1997
Text copyright © Field Enterprises Educational Corporation, 1965
Reprinted by permission of World Books, Inc. Original title "I Speak, I Say, I Talk."
All rights reserved

THE LIBRARY OF CONGRESS HAS CATALOGED THE G. P. PUTNAM'S SONS EDITION AS FOLLOWS:
Shapiro, Arnold, date Mice squeak, We speak/by Arnold L. Shapiro; illustrated by Tomie dePaola. p. cm.
Summary: Illustrations and simple text describe the ways various animals communicate,
such as "Owls hoot," "Pigs squeal," and "Bees buzz."
[1. Animal sounds—Fiction.] I. dePaola, Tomie, ill. II. Title.
PZ7.S5294Mi 1997 [E]—dc21 96-54895 CIP AC
ISBN 0-399-23202-8

This edition ISBN 0-698-11873-1

Printed in the United States of America
Designed by Patrick Collins and Donna Mark. Lettering by David Gatti.